Emily and the Enchanted Frog

by
HELEN V. GRIFFITH

pictures by
SUSAN CONDIE LAMB

Greenwillow Books New York

FOR THE REAL EMILY

Watercolor paints and pen-and-ink were used for
the full-color art. The text type is Palatino.

Text copyright © 1989 by Helen V. Griffith
Illustrations copyright © 1989 by Susan Condie Lamb
All rights reserved. No part of this book
may be reproduced or utilized in any form
or by any means, electronic or mechanical,
including photocopying, recording or by
any information storage and retrieval
system, without permission in writing
from the Publisher, Greenwillow Books,
a division of William Morrow & Company, Inc.,
105 Madison Avenue, New York, N.Y. 10016.

First Edition   10 9 8 7 6 5 4 3 2 1

Library of Congress Cataloging-in-Publication Data
Griffith, Helen V.
Emily and the enchanted frog / by Helen V. Griffith
pictures by Susan Condie Lamb.
p.   cm.
Contents: Emily and the elf—
Emily and the mermaid—
Emily and the enchanted frog.
ISBN 0-688-08483-4.   ISBN 0-688-08484-2 (lib. bdg.),
[1. Wishes—Fiction.   2. Crabs—Fiction.
3. Frogs—Fiction.]
I. Lamb, Susan Condie, ill.
II. Title.   PZ7.G8823Em 1989
[E]—dc19   88-16511   CIP   AC

Printed in Singapore by Tien Wah Press

CONTENTS

EMILY and the ENCHANTED FROG

One day Emily was walking beside a pond. She saw a frog sitting on a rock staring into space. It seemed sad.

"I'll bet that is an enchanted frog," Emily thought. "I'll bet a wicked witch has cast a spell on a handsome prince and turned him into that frog. And I'll bet the only way that frog can turn back into a handsome prince is for a beautiful maiden to kiss him. He's lucky I came along."

She picked up the frog and kissed it on the lips. Sure enough, she had hardly finished yelling "Yuck!" and wiping her mouth on her sleeve before the frog was gone and a handsome prince was standing in its place.

"What's the big idea?" said the handsome prince.

He didn't sound very grateful. In fact, he didn't sound grateful at all.

"Thanks to me you are no longer an ugly frog," Emily said.

"I never was an ugly frog," said the prince. "I was a handsome frog. Now look at me. Ugh."

Emily was surprised. Maybe he had been a frog so long that he'd forgotten he had ever been a prince.

"Don't you remember a wicked witch casting a spell on you?" she asked.

"Don't remind me," said the prince.

"Well, I just broke the spell," said Emily.

"What gives you that idea?" asked the prince.

He seemed to be a very slow-thinking prince.

"You had to remain a frog until a beautiful maiden came along and kissed you. It's a fairly common spell," said Emily.

"There was nothing in the spell about a beautiful maiden," said the prince. "Anybody would do."

Emily felt a little disappointed at that, but she said, "Well, anyway, I broke the spell, didn't I? You can go back to your royal family and the royal life you led before you were enchanted."

"You've got it backwards," said the prince. "In real life I am a frog. According to the spell, if someone came along and kissed me, I would no longer be a frog, but would have to live out my days as a handsome prince. What a horrible fate."

"Being a handsome prince isn't so horrible," Emily said. "Lots of people would like to be handsome princes."

"People, maybe. Not frogs," said the prince. "Frogs are used to a life of diving and swimming."

"Princes do that," said Emily.

"And sitting in the sun," said the prince.

"They do that, too," said Emily.

"And catching bugs with their tongues," said the prince.

"You may have to give that up," said Emily.

The prince sat down on a rock and sighed.

"A frog's greatest joy is catching bugs with its tongue," he said.

He watched a little beetle hurrying through the grass.

"Maybe you'll like being a prince," Emily said to take his mind off the beetle.

"Never," said the prince.

He leaned over and looked at himself in the pond.

"You don't realize how ugly people are until you see them close up," he said.

Emily had never thought a handsome prince could get on her nerves, but this one did.

"Well, I have to go now," she said.

"Wait a minute," said the prince. "First you have to help me break this spell."

"Is that possible?" Emily asked.

"There's only one way," said the prince. "I must be kissed by a beautiful princess."

"In that case I can't help," said Emily. "I don't know any beautiful princesses."

"Just any old beautiful princess won't work, anyway," said the prince. "She has to be a beautiful princess who is really a frog who has been turned into a beautiful princess by a magic spell."

"Could you repeat that?" Emily asked.

"Somewhere in this pond there is a frog who is under the same horrible spell I'm under," said the prince. "If kissed by a person, she will become a (ugh) beautiful princess. But then, if she and I find each other and kiss, our spells will be broken. We will turn back into frogs and live happily ever after."

"And what do you want me to do, as if I didn't know?" Emily said.

"Just kiss the other enchanted frog, that's all," said the prince.

"I'd really like to help," Emily said, "but I don't see any frogs around right now."

Actually, she didn't want to kiss another frog, but she didn't like to say that. So she looked behind a couple of rocks and said, "Nope, no frogs. Too bad."

"I know where they hide," said the prince. "I may look like a person (ugh) but inside I am all frog."

The prince was right about knowing frogs. In no time he found one and held it out to Emily. She could see that he would never be happy until he was free of his spell, so she gave the frog a kiss. Nothing happened.

"Wrong frog," said the prince.

He caught another frog and then another one, and Emily kissed each one. By the time she had kissed a dozen or so, her lips felt very strange. And all the frogs were still frogs.

"Do you expect me to kiss every frog in this pond?" Emily asked.

"Just until one turns into a beautiful princess," said the prince.

"How do you know someone hasn't already come along and kissed the other frog?" Emily asked.

"I don't," said the prince.

He grabbed another frog.

"You mean I might be doing this for nothing?" Emily yelled.

The prince didn't answer. He was having trouble holding onto the frog he had just caught.

"Quick," he said, and Emily kissed the frog.

Right before their eyes it turned into a beautiful princess.

"At last," said Emily.

"Thanks a lot," the beautiful princess said angrily.

"It's okay," said the prince. "I am also a frog, under the same horrible spell you are under."

"Sure you are," said the princess.

"It's true," said the prince. "All we have to do is kiss each other and we'll be frogs again and live happily ever after."

"How do I know that?" asked the princess.

"That's just the way the spell works," said the prince. "Didn't the witch explain it to you?"

"Yes," said the princess, "but how do I know this isn't a trick? How do I know you're really a frog? And how can I bring myself to (ugh) kiss a person?"

"Listen," Emily said, "if I can kiss all those frogs, you can kiss one handsome prince."

"What have you got to lose?" asked the prince. "Do you want to go through life looking like that?"

The princess looked at herself in the pond and shuddered. "Pucker up," she said.

The beautiful princess and the handsome prince closed their eyes tightly and kissed the world's shortest kiss. Instantly they turned into frogs.

Emily watched them hop away side by side. She was happy for them. She was happy for herself, too, knowing that she had kissed her last frog.

As they leaped along, one of the frogs flipped out its tongue and snagged a bug.

It did look kind of fun at that.

EMILY
and the ELF

Emily was almost asleep one night when an elf appeared on her pillow.

"I've come to grant you a wish," he said.

Emily sat up.

"Just one?" she asked. "Isn't it usually three?"

"Don't be greedy," said the elf. "What's your wish?"

Emily had often thought what she would want if she could have her wish, so she was prepared.

"I wish to be invisible," she said.

"Really?" said the elf. "Most people want a million dollars or a pony."

"They would have been my other two wishes," said Emily.

"Well, your wish is granted," said the elf, and he vanished.

Emily hopped out of bed and looked in the mirror. There was enough light to see that she wasn't there. Even her nightgown was invisible.

"This is going to be fun," she said.

Emily got back into bed to think about all the things she could do now that she was invisible.

"The first thing I'll do is sneak up on the cat," she thought.

Emily had never been able to sneak up on the cat.

"But he won't know who's grabbing him," she thought. "He might scratch me."

Emily decided she'd better not sneak up on the cat.

"I'll be good at games, though," she thought.
"Nobody will be able to catch me."

Then she thought, "But they won't even
know I'm playing."

Emily decided games wouldn't
be much fun after all.

"Well, it will be nice to be invisible
in school," she thought. "I'll never
get called on, because the teacher
won't know I'm there."

Then she thought,
"But if she doesn't know I'm there,
she'll mark me absent every day."

Other bad things about being
invisible came to her mind:

"If I'm not careful,
people will sit on me."

"If I don't watch out,
birds will fly into me."

"Grandmother won't know
how big to knit my sweaters."

"And how will I get my hair cut?"

"Why didn't I think of these things
before?" Emily wondered.

She got out of bed and looked in the mirror again. She still wasn't there.

"I don't think I'm going to like being invisible," she thought.

Emily went to the window and looked for the elf, but there was no sign of him.

"I'll just have to make the best of it," she decided.

She climbed back into bed and tried to think of something good about being invisible.

She couldn't.

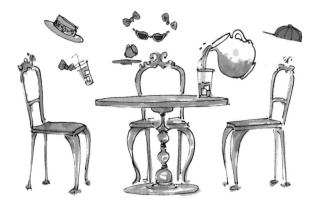

"Maybe there are other invisible people," she thought. "We could get together and talk about our problems."

Emily imagined a room full of invisible people talking together. The thought made her laugh. While she was laughing the elf appeared.

"There you are," he said. "I've been looking for you everywhere."

"I'm invisible, remember?" said Emily.

"That's what I want to talk to you about," said the elf. "There's been a mistake. You weren't supposed to get a wish."

"What luck," said Emily.

"You were supposed to get three," said the elf.

"Oh no," said Emily.

"Now you can have the million dollars and the pony," said the elf.

"Wait," said Emily. "First I want to unwish my first wish."

"You mean you want to be uninvisible?" asked the elf.

"Yes," said Emily.

"Granted," said the elf.

Emily hopped up and looked in the mirror.

"There I am," she said.

"You get one more wish," said the elf. "What will it be?"

"I'm not sure," said Emily. "Either the million dollars or the pony."

Emily thought for a long time.

Sometimes she wanted the money.

Sometimes she wanted the pony.

The elf was getting bored.

"Wish for the money," he said. "Then you can use some to buy a pony."

"A bought pony isn't the same as a wished pony," said Emily.

She thought some more.

"I wish I could make up my mind," she said, and right away she knew what she wanted.

"I'll take the pony," she said.

"That's four wishes," said the elf. "You only get three."

"I only made three wishes," said Emily. "To be invisible, to be visible—"

"And to make up your mind. That's three wishes," said the elf, and he disappeared.

When Emily thought it over she could see that he was right. For a few minutes she was disappointed. Then she thought, "Well, I've had three wishes. And they all came true."

She got into bed again.

"Anyway," she thought, "if the elf ever comes back, I'll know that wish number one is for a pony. And wish number two is for a million dollars. But what shall I use my other wish for?"

Emily lay awake for a long time trying to decide on wish number three. She fell asleep before she made up her mind.

EMILY and the MERMAID

One day Emily found a shell on the beach.

"That looks like a listening shell," she said.

"If I hold that shell up to my ear, I'll hear the ocean."

She put the shell against her ear and listened.

"Put me down," said a voice.

"That's not the ocean," said Emily.

She looked inside the shell.

Two black eyes were looking back.

"I was just trying to hear the ocean," said Emily.

"There's no ocean in here," said the voice.

Emily put the shell back on the sand.

She lay on her stomach and looked in at the two black eyes.

"Are you a crab?" she asked.

"Heavens no," said the voice.

"A spider, maybe?" Emily asked.

A shriek came from the shell.

"I'm afraid of spiders," said the voice.

"I'm sorry," said Emily.

She tried to think of something less scary.

"Would you be an oyster?" she asked.

"I would not," said the voice. "What I am is a mermaid."

"A mermaid!" said Emily. "I've never seen a mermaid."

Emily really didn't think a mermaid would be living in a little shell.

"But you never know," she thought to herself, and out loud she said, "Can you come out?"

She sat up and waited hopefully, and after a moment a little creature scrambled out of the shell and onto the sand. It had two black eyes on stalks, lots of legs, and one big claw.

"Where's the mermaid?" Emily asked.

"I'm the mermaid," said the creature.

"You're not a mermaid," said Emily.

"You said you'd never seen one," said the creature.

"I've seen pictures," said Emily. "Mermaids have long golden hair."

"They do?" said the creature.

"And they have fish tails," said Emily.

"They do?" said the creature.

"And they don't live in shells," said Emily.

"They don't?" said the creature.

"No," said Emily. "They don't."

The creature sat very still for a minute.

Then it put its claw over its face and began to cry.

"What's the matter?" asked Emily.

"I'm not a mermaid," cried the creature.

"Well, neither am I," said Emily. "Do you see me crying about it?"

"I thought sure I was a mermaid," cried the creature.

Emily began to be sorry she had said anything. She wondered how she could cheer the creature up.

"Do you know what I think?" she said. "I don't think there are any mermaids."

The creature looked at Emily through its claw.

"No mermaids?" it said.

"They're just a nice idea," said Emily.

The creature put down its claw and sniffed.

"If there aren't any mermaids," it said, "I must be something else."

"I would think so," said Emily.

"I wonder what," said the creature.

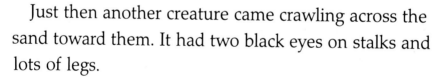

Just then another creature came crawling across the sand toward them. It had two black eyes on stalks and lots of legs.

"It looks just like you," said Emily. "Now we can find out what you are."

"I hope I'm something nice," said the creature.

"We have a question," Emily said to the other creature. "Are you a clam?"

"No, I'm a mermaid," said the other creature. "Is this shell taken?"

"Mermaids don't live in shells," said Emily.

"They most certainly do," said the other creature.

"Mermaids have long golden hair and fish tails," said Emily.

"They most certainly don't," said the other creature.

"I've seen pictures," said Emily.

"I don't know what those pictures were of," said the other creature, "but they weren't mermaids."

It crawled into the listening shell and scuttled away.

The little creature burst into tears. "It took my shell," it cried.

"I never knew mermaids were such crybabies," said Emily.

The creature stopped crying. "Did you say I was a mermaid?" it asked.

"I'll say this," said Emily. "If that other creature was a mermaid, then you're a mermaid."

The little creature wiggled its feelers happily.

"I didn't like not being a mermaid," it said.

Emily and the creature strolled along the beach together.
"Look," said Emily, "here's another listening shell."
"Mermaid shell," said the creature.
It settled itself inside the shell and looked out at Emily.
"Isn't it funny," it said. "You never saw a mermaid
before, and today you've seen two."